AND THE
END
OF THE
WORLD

PaRragon

Bath · New York · Singapore · Hong Kong · Cologne · Delhi · Melbourne

Written by Zed Storm
Creative concept and words by E. Hawken
Check out the website at www.will-solvit.com

First edition published by Parragon in 2010

Parragon
Queen Street House
4 Queen Street
Bath BA1 1HE, UK

ISBN 978-1-4454-0460-8

Printed in China.

Please retain this information for future reference.

CONTENTS

Blast off!

WOOHOO

"What do monsters have on their toast?" I asked Zoe through a mouthful of fried egg.

She shrugged at me and bit into buttered toast.

"Scream cheese!" I said.

Zoe laughed and nearly spat her toast all over the kitchen table.

"Will, no joke-telling with your mouth full, please," Mum said with a frown, spooning another helping of egg onto my plate.

I looked up and gave Mum a huge smile. This was the first breakfast time I'd had with Mum in months. She'd been missing for ages, you see. I found her in a time vortex on an island in the middle of the sea.

Scream cheese!
Hee hee!

aarrgghh!

It was nice not to be force-fed kippers with jam for breakfast. Usually it's Grandpa Monty who does the cooking, and he'd never cook anything as normal as bacon and eggs on toast.

"What time is your mother coming to pick you up, Zoe?" Mum asked my best friend. Zoe had slept over in the spare room the night before.

"Mum'll just pick me up from school later today," Zoe replied, biting into a juicy piece of bacon that oozed grease down her chin.

"It's a school day today?" Mum said, surprised. "Wow, being in a time vortex for hundreds of years really makes you lose track of the days of the week!"

"Is that bacon and eggs I smell?" Grandpa Monty's nose twitched as he hobbled into the kitchen on his walking stick. "Urgh!" he screwed his face up. "Disgusting stuff!"

I reached down and sneakily gave Plato, Grandpa's small white dog, a piece of bacon. Plato wagged his tail and then looked up at me, begging for more.

"So," I said, letting out a loud belch. Mum looked at me disapprovingly. "What's the plan? We need to rescue Dad!" Mum had promised that we could set out to find my dad as soon as we'd had breakfast, and I was desperate to get this Adventure under way.

"Well, I hadn't realized it was a school day," Mum replied, half looking at me and half looking at Grandpa as he began to fry kippers in jam.

"Who cares if it's a school day?" I shrugged.

"I care," Zoe said quietly.

Trust Zoe to be a total geek about school!

"I care too," Mum said firmly. "No more Adventures until you're back from school."

9

"But, Mum..."

"No 'buts', Will!" she argued. "School first, Adventures later."

"So not fair!" I muttered, getting up from my seat and heading out of the kitchen.

I quickly ran upstairs, washed, got dressed and packed up my school bag.

I put my diary of adventure clues and Grandpa Monty's spy diary in my bag. Believe me, there was no way I could pay attention in class when my dad still needed rescuing. Reading through my clue book and Grandpa's diary would be a much better use of my time!

"Will!" I heard Mum call from downstairs. "Time for school!"

I ran down the staircase, taking two steps at a time and dashing past the portraits of all my Adventurer ancestors.

Everyone born into my family is an Adventurer. Adventurers get sent mysterious letters that give us clues to mysteries we have to solve and people we have to help. Every Adventurer has a special skill, and my special skill is time travelling.

Zoe was waiting for me at the bottom of the staircase. "Stanley's going to drive us to school," she said.

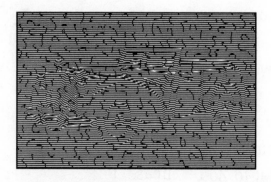

"Cool," I said as Mum gave me a goodbye kiss on the cheek.

Stanley is Grandpa Monty's driver and butler, although I'm sure he does other stuff too. I'm not sure what kind of stuff he does – but I know he used to work for the President!

Zoe and I walked towards Stanley's car and climbed into the back seats.

"Did you bring your clue diary with you?" Zoe asked me as Stanley drove down Solvit Hall's mile-long driveway.

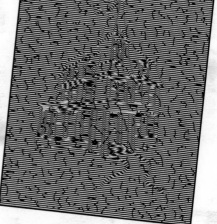

I dug my hand into my backpack and pulled out my diary, passing it to Zoe.

She opened it and started to read my new clues.

THE DIARY AND CLUE RECORD OF WILL SOLVIT, TIME TRAVELLING ADVENTURER

CLUES

- Mum and Dad were separated in time and space.
- The alien race Partek were holding Mum prisoner in a time vortex so they could trap me when I came to rescue her.
- The Partek figured out a better plan to trap me so just abandoned Mum.
- Dad is in the future.
- My last letter told me to 'Voyage to the end of time'.

While Zoe was busy, I read through Grandpa's spy diary. Grandpa Monty's special Adventuring skill was spying, and he kept an awesome diary about all the cool things he used to do.

8th February 1954

After a short period disguised as a Russian miner, I've arrived in China. My plan is simple – dig an underground tunnel to take me to the secret bunker and smuggle stolen gold out from under the city.

I've taken a shovel, a battery-powered torch and a case to put the gold in.

I suspect it will be cold under the ground, and I intend to spend at least three weeks digging the tunnel. I plan to keep myself warm by wearing my Arctic fleece and drinking dandelion juice.

I never knew that dandelion juice kept you warm – I'm always picking up great tips from Grandpa Monty's diary!

Stanley dropped us off at the school gates as the bell was ringing.

"You're late," Mrs Jones snarled as Zoe and I ran into the classroom.

"Sorry, Mrs Jones," Zoe said as we sat down.

"Today, class," our teacher said, "we're going to be learning about rockets. Please turn to page 189 of your physics text book and read the instructions for home-made rockets."

COOL! I thought.

Physics lessons were usually DULL! But building rockets sounded awesome.

SO COOL!

In case you're wondering, this is a good way to make a home-made rocket:

1. Cut out a length of cardboard and glue it into a tube shape.
2. Wrap and tape the tube around an old film canister.
3. Tape fins to your rocket body.
4. Roll a circle of paper into a cone and tape it to the rocket's top.
5. Put on your eye protection.
6. Turn the rocket upside down.
7. Fill the canister one-third full of water.
8. Drop one-half of an effervescing vitamin tablet into the canister.
9. Snap the canister lid on tight.
10. Stand your rocket on a launch platform.
11. Stand back and wait. Your rocket will blast off!

The classroom went crazy! There were rockets blasting all over the place – I don't think Mrs Jones had thought the lesson through properly because it was chaos!

F.U.N!!!

My rocket whizzed off through an open window and got caught in a bush just outside.

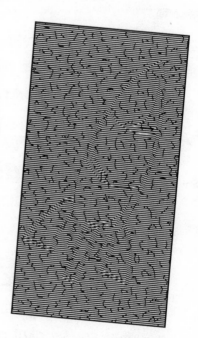

I ran over to the window to get it back.

But my rocket wasn't the only thing waiting in the bush.

There was a letter, too.

A letter with my name on it!

WHERE DO ASTRONAUTS KEEP THEIR SPACESHIPS?
AT PARKING METEORS!

YOUR BIGGEST ADVENTURE YET IS ABOUT TO BEGIN.
TO FIND YOUR FATHER, YOU MUST TRAVEL AS FAR INTO
THE FUTURE AS YOU CAN. YOU'LL FIND HIM AT THE
VERY END OF THE KNOWN UNIVERSE.

TAKE AS MANY FRIENDS AS YOU CAN. THE BEST
ADVENTURERS ARE THOSE WHO KNOW WHEN THEY CAN
WORK ALONE, AND WHEN THEY MUST SUMMON AN ARMY.

START WITH AN ANCESTOR WHO'S EXPECTING TO SEE
YOU AGAIN SOON...

Always rings at the wrong time!

"Well, the ancestor who's expecting to see you again is obviously Captain Luke Solvit," Zoe said, biting into an apple at lunchtime.

"Obviously," I agreed. I'd recently met Captain Luke when I time travelled back to 1804 to rescue Mum. "But what about the others? Who else can help me?"

The school bell rang, interrupting us.

"The last place I wanna be right now is falling asleep in a French lesson when I should be rescuing my dad," I complained as we walked towards French class.

"Who knows," Zoe grinned at me, "maybe you'll need to speak French in this Adventure?"

"Doubtful!" I whinged.

That afternoon was officially the longest in the history of time – fact. I seriously hoped that I didn't have to use French on this Adventure, cuz I didn't pay attention to anything the teacher was saying! The whole lesson went in one ear and out the next.

As soon as school was over I belted towards the school gates at the speed of a rocket. "I'll IM you later," Zoe called after me.

"OK," I called back, running to meet Stanley.

Grandpa's driver hardly ever speaks, but I had a few things on my mind. As he was the only one in the car with me, I decided to pick his brains...

"In your experience, Stanley," I asked, "what kind of people do you need to form an army?"

"Soldiers?" Stanley asked in his cool-as-ice voice.

"Not exactly," I said. I tried to explain a bit better. "I need to summon an Adventurer army."

"So you need people with Adventurer skills?"

he asked.

"Yeah," I agreed.

"So you'll need people who can fight, people who can carry you to battle, people who have the means to find out where the battle is…"

I knew Stanley would be an awesome person to ask for advice.

We drove down the mile-long driveway to Solvit Hall. The driveway was lined with stone statues of previous Adventurers, and I gazed at each one as we passed, wondering who might be useful in my Adventurer army.

Mum was waiting for me at the front door of Solvit Hall. "Do you have homework to do?" she asked as I hung up my coat.

"Yeah," I said. "I'll get it done before dinner."

"I'm cooking fish-egg and baked-potato ice cream," Grandpa Monty called from the kitchen.

Yeuck!!

Mum drew her eyebrows together and let out a sigh. "He insisted on doing the cooking," she whispered to me.

"Easy on the fish eggs," I called back to Grandpa. "And after dinner we'll go and find Dad," I said to Mum, heading towards the staircase. "You promised, remember."

"I remember," she called after me.

Plato followed me up the stairs and jumped on my bed as I slammed my bedroom door behind me.

I pulled my clue diary out of my school bag and opened it at a blank page. I started to write a list of all the people I'd met during my Adventures who might be useful for my army.

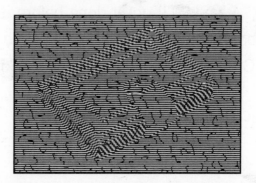

NAME:	SKILL:	LOCATION:
Captain Luke Solvit	Airship fleet commander	1804
Captain Drake	Space pilot	The DARE Satellite
Mark Antony	Army General	Ancient Rome
Akemi the samurai warrior	Amazing fighter	Ancient Japan
Lord Avalon	Understands the Talisman of Truth better than I do	Avalon Castle, medieval times
Jamie Solvit	Space explorer	Solvit Hall in the future
Grandpa Monty	Spy	Solvit Hall, present time
Zoe	Ace at cracking codes	Zoe's mum's house

"Dinner!" Mum called from downstairs.

Plato barked, leaped off the bed and started scratching at my bedroom door.

"All right, all right," I said to Plato. I don't know what he was so excited about – he hated Grandpa Monty's cooking as much as I did!

Plato and I nearly tripped over each other as we ran down the stairs. Clutching my clue diary, I burst into the kitchen and announced my plan to Mum and Grandpa. "After dinner we have to travel through time and space to forge an army."

"Wash your hands," Mum said, laying plates around the table.

I dropped my diary onto the table and gave my hands a wash in the kitchen sink.

"Hungry?" Grandpa beamed at me. "I've made lots!"

He slopped the ice cream onto my plate.

Muu–uuum!

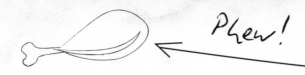

Phew!

Thankfully Mum had also made a roast chicken to eat. "Growing boys can't just eat ice cream," she said to Grandpa Monty as he gave her a disapproving look.

"So," I said, tucking into my chicken. "I had a letter today telling me I had to summon an army to rescue Dad."

"Let me see," Mum said, as if she didn't believe me. I pulled the letter out of my pocket and passed it to Mum. "Hmmm," she murmured as she read, "what scruffy handwriting."

Trust Mum to comment on handwriting at a time like this!

"I've made a list of people I think would be good in the army," I announced. "It's all people who have helped me out in other Adventures, so I know they'll be good to have around this time."

I read out the list I'd written in between

mouthfuls of dinner.

"Me?" Grandpa Monty said, looking chuffed.

"Yes, Grandpa," I said, smiling at him.

"It's been a while since I had an Adventure," he said.

"I'm sure you'll remember how it's done," I assured him.

Plato yapped loudly from underneath the table. "You can come too, boy," Grandpa said to Plato. Plato wagged his tail excitedly.

"So, plan of action…" I said, finishing the last of the chicken on my plate. "Collect Zoe and then time travel to pick everyone else up."

"How will all these people fit in a time machine?" Grandpa asked, spooning a large mouthful of ice cream between his lips.

"Oh, I hadn't thought of that," I admitted, slumping back into my chair with disappointment.

This may be harder than I thought it would be.

"Morph is fuelled by dark energy," Mum said simply. "Dark energy allows it to grow into whatever size it needs to be. We can fit as many people as you want in there!"

"Awesome!" I smiled – the more I knew about dark energy, the more amazing it was. I couldn't wait to get Dad back to tell me even more!

Something in my pocket began to buzz. BUZZ BUZZ

I pulled out my SurfM8 to read the message. BUZZ

"No phones at the dinner table, Will," Mum said.

"Mum! It's not a phone, it's a SurfM8." Wow – mums can be SO uncool!

I quickly read the IM that Zoe had sent me and IM'd her back.

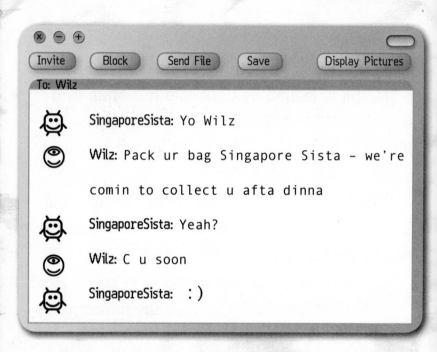

SingaporeSista: Yo Wilz

Wilz: Pack ur bag Singapore Sista - we're comin to collect u afta dinna

SingaporeSista: Yeah?

Wilz: C u soon

SingaporeSista: :)

After dinner I quickly threw together my best Adventure tools:

Stun gun
Supersonic screecher
Morph's discs

Compass that always points home
Invisibility paint
Walkie-talkie earplugs
Omnilumes
Super-strength fart gas
Samurai sword

That's when I saw the jewelled mask that I'd
been given by the
Ancient Aztecs. The
mask that makes the
wearer invincible.

The mask terrified
me. I'd seen
first-hand what that
kind of power can
do to someone – it
makes them mad.

But my father had sent a message to me via Mutex, who used to own the mask, saying that one day I'd need it.

If there was ever a time for invincibility – that time was now.

I packed the mask away with my other tools and closed my bag.

"Will, are you ready?" Mum called.

Mum and Grandpa Monty were standing by the front door in their coats. Plato was wagging his tail beside them. Grandpa was clutching a picnic basket. "Food for the Adventure," he smiled.

I think most of my army would rather go hungry than eat Grandpa Monty's food!

"Stanley's going to drive us over to Zoe's mum's house," Mum told me. "We'll take Morph from there."

"Sure thing," I said.

We headed towards the car where Stanley was waiting for us.

This is it, I thought. My greatest Adventure is about to begin.

Stanley is soooooo cool!!

CHAPTER THREE
ARMY RECRUITMENT

Zoe was waiting by the front door as Stanley's car pulled up at her house. "Hi, Mrs Solvit," she waved at Mum.

Mum waved back then turned to me and whispered, "She's ever such a pretty girl."

OMG, Mum! So embarrassing!!

Zoe climbed into the car. "I've told Mum you're taking me to the circus," she said.

"The circus?" I said sceptically.

"Yeah," Zoe replied, putting on her seatbelt. "Mum wasn't keen on letting me go out on a school night but I said that the circus is only in town for one night and that you'd kindly offered to take me along."

"We're going to a circus?" Grandpa Monty said hopefully from the passenger seat at the front.

"No, Monty," Mum said, as if she was cross with him. "Zoe just said we were going to the circus so her mum wouldn't get suspicious."

"So where are we going?" Grandpa asked.

"We're going to rescue Dad, remember?" I answered. "We're going to travel in time to collect an army of Adventurers and then we're going to travel to the end of the universe to find Dad."

Grandpa let out an irritated grunt. "I'd rather have gone to the circus."

Stanley drove us to a quiet country lane and stopped the car.

"Everybody out," I instructed.

Grandpa Monty and Plato clambered out of the front of the car and Mum, Zoe and I got out of the back.

"We'll be back as soon as possible, Stanley," I said as I closed the car door.

"I'll meet you back at Solvit Hall," Stanley told Grandpa. "If you need me, you know how to call me – no matter where you are."

"What does that mean?" I asked.

"Do they have lions at this circus?" Grandpa asked, changing the subject. He obviously didn't want me to discover the secrets he and Stanley had between them.

I pulled Morph out of my backpack. It was still in the shape of a mini time machine from the last time I used it. Morph's lights flickered on as soon as I touched it and it began to spin around and expand into a full-sized time machine.

"After you," I smiled at Mum, opening the time machine door for her.

Totally mega gadget! 34

Mum, Zoe, Grandpa Monty, Plato and I all piled into Morph.

Mum was right – Morph had always seemed just about big enough for two to three people. But it didn't feel like a squeeze at all with four of us plus a dog in there. Morph seemed to grow into whatever size it needed to be.

"Where are we going first?" Zoe asked, shuffling towards the time machine control panel.

Before she could even press a button, Morph had begun to move through time.

"What's going on?" Mum shrieked.

"Morph does this a lot," I said, trying not to puke as Morph spun us through time. "It just seems to take us where we need to go without being programmed."

The time machine jolted to a halt. "Are we there?" Zoe asked with a hand over her mouth, as if she was about to chuck-up all over the place.

Plato let out a loud growl – time travelling is as rough for dogs as it is for humans.

"Will Solvit?" called a voice from outside the time machine.

"Captain Luke!" Zoe shouted, rushing towards the time machine door and flinging it open.

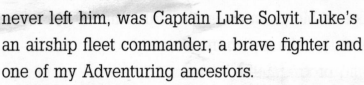

There, standing in a field, as if we'd never left him, was Captain Luke Solvit. Luke's an airship fleet commander, a brave fighter and one of my Adventuring ancestors.

"Good day, Zoe," Luke beamed, shaking Zoe's hand. "Mrs Solvit, Will," he said to Mum and me.

"This is Grandpa Monty," I said, introducing Grandpa. "And this is Plato."

Captain Luke bent down and gave Plato a good fur ruffle before standing up and asking me, "So, what's the plan for Adventure?"

"The plan," I said simply, "is to get in my time machine and go and rescue my dad."

"Fantastic," Luke smiled. "I've wanted to time travel ever since we first met."

"First we need to collect the rest of our army," Zoe told Luke.

"Army?" he frowned.

"Yes, you're the first one to join." This made Captain Luke stand up a bit taller and pull his shoulders back with pride.

"Take me to the Adventure," he said, grinning.

We all piled back into Morph – there were six of us now, including Plato.

Once again, Morph began spinning and zooming through time.

The next stop was ancient Rome. We met Mark Antony on the steps of the Roman Senate. "Will Solvit," he greeted me warmly.

"I need your help in battle," I told him.

"I'll fight with you to the death!" he replied.

With Mark Antony, the great Roman army general, on board, Morph began whizzing through time once again.

We arrived on a mountaintop in Japan. Akemi, a member of the Army of the Sun samurai warriors, was practising chopping through wood with his bare hands.

"Hi, Akemi!" Zoe called, as we left everyone else behind in Morph and ran towards him.

"Zoe, Will!" Akemi said fondly.

We quickly explained why we had come and

that we needed Akemi to join our army.

"Of course, young Adventurer," Akemi bowed. "Let me collect my sword and then we will travel to the end of the world."

As soon as Akemi had his sword and had said goodbye to Shinobi and the other samurai

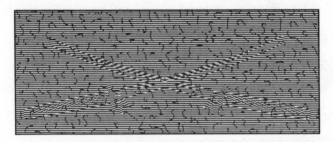

warriors, we time travelled once again.

The next stop was Avalon Castle in medieval times. Morph landed in the castle courtyard where Egbert the dragon was helping Barnaby the knight light a fire.

"Will!" Barnaby shouted.

"It's awesome to see you guys," I said, "but I'm here for Lord Avalon."

Barnaby led me through the dark halls of Avalon Castle and up the winding staircase to Lord Avalon's room.

"I will of course help you with your Adventure, Will," Lord Avalon said after we explained our mission.

Lord Avalon climbed into the time machine with me, Mum, Zoe, Plato, Grandpa Monty, Captain Luke, Mark Antony and Akemi.

"Next stop – outer space!" I said.

Morph took us back to the present day and then turned into a space rocket and blasted us towards the DARE Satellite.

The DARE Satellite was just as I'd remembered it. Everything was stark white and there were hundreds of scientists in white lab coats

It was soooo cool seeing them all again!

everywhere.

"I'd be proud to come aboard your ship," Captain Drake told me.

"Only one more person to collect and the army is complete," I told everyone aboard. "This person is going to help us Adventure to the end of the known universe."

Morph journeyed through time and space and took us to Jamie Solvit at Solvit Hall in the future.

"Will!" Jamie said, smiling.

"I need your help," I told him.

"I'll help you with whatever you need," he agreed.

I finally had everyone I needed. I'd done just as the letter had told me to do – I'd summoned an army.

Now all I had to do was take my army into battle and rescue my dad!

CHAPTER FOUR
BOB THE ROBOT

"So, let me get this right," Jamie said as Morph began to whizz forward in time. "You've been told by whoever writes your letters that you need to summon an army to take with you as far into the future as you can go. Then you have to travel to the end of the known universe to rescue your father."

"Sounds crazy, doesn't it?" I answered.

Thankfully, Jamie was a Solvit Adventurer, just like me. Otherwise, he might have thought I was bonkers.

"So how far into the future can Morph go?" he asked.

OLL! Nooo!

I shrugged. I honestly had no idea.

"I'm going to feed the troops with some banana and egg sandwiches I made for the journey," Grandpa informed me, foraging around in his picnic basket.

"Go for it," I said, trying not to gag at the thought of egg and banana together. "I'm not hungry though."

Jamie and I walked to the front of the time machine (by now Morph had stretched into a huge machine that you could walk around in, and the ride was much smoother than usual).

"What do you think will be waiting for us at the end of time and space?" Jamie asked.

"Who knows?" I replied. "All I know is that I have the best army for whatever lies ahead."

Morph ground to a halt.

We had arrived at the furthest date in the

future that a time machine can travel to.

"Will," Zoe said, walking up to me. "Is this it? Are we here? At the end of time?"

"Wherever we are, it's where Morph thinks we need to be. And Morph is never wrong."

"I shall lead the way!" Mark Antony declared, raising his Roman sword above his head. Mark Antony doesn't speak in English – he speaks in Latin. I'm not mega-brainy, but I can understand Latin. In fact, I can understand any language. I wear an amulet called the Talisman of Truth that translates things for me.

I translated Mark Antony's words to the others: "He wants to lead the way."

"No, sir, I shall lead the way," argued Captain Luke, pushing Mark Antony to the side.

"I can ride the wind, I shall go first," argued Akemi.

Great! I thought. Too many leaders and not enough followers!

"This is Will's army," said Captain Drake. "We shall follow him."

"Well said, Drake," said Mum. "Henry was always right about you – you're a good guy to have around in a crisis."

"OK," I said, making my way to the time machine door. "I'll go out first and see what's there. It's probably best if everyone is prepared to fight – we don't know what's going to be waiting for us outside. So grab a weapon or anything that you can protect yourself with."

I dug around in my backpack and handed an Adventure tool to anyone who didn't already have a weapon. I gave super-strength fart gas to Grandpa, an omnilume to Zoe, the supersonic screecher to Mum and my stun gun to Lord

I'm not sure he really needs it!

45

Avalon. I kept the Aztec mask of invincibility for myself.

Taking a deep breath, I slowly opened the time machine door.

The whistle of wind stung my ears.

Morph had landed in a wasteland. The soil was bare, there was rubbish everywhere and the sky was dark.

My footsteps crunched down on the ground as I stepped out of the time machine.

If this was the future, it was a pretty horrible place.

Everyone followed behind me, and I led them out into the wasteland.

The wind pushed small chunks of scrap metal over the ground. It was disgusting – it was as if thousands of years of junk and garbage had just been left to rot and pile on top of themselves.

I could see blinking lights in the distance.

"What's that?" called Lord Avalon. "A candle?"

"Something tells me it isn't a candle," I replied with suspicion.

I led the way towards the flickering lights.

As we got nearer, I could see that there were two lights. They looked like eyes sitting in a metal face.

A robot.

The robot was shaped like a human. He was wearing a black bow tie and a smart suit on top of his

He was a little bit freaky!!

metallic body.

His arms were outstretched as if he was carrying a tray. But instead of a tray in his hands there was a white envelope.

The envelope had my name on it.

DID YOU HEAR ABOUT THE MAD SCIENTIST WHO PUT DYNAMITE IN HIS FRIDGE?

THEY SAY HE BLEW HIS COOL!

THIS IS BOB. BOB WILL TELL YOU WHAT YOU NEED TO KNOW. ALL YOU NEED TO DO IS ASK. FIRST YOU MUST TURN BOB ON. TO DO SO, TYPE THE ANSWER TO THIS QUESTION INTO THE KEYBOARD IN THE BACK OF BOB'S HEAD:

THERE WERE TWO DUCKS IN FRONT OF A DUCK AND TWO DUCKS BEHIND A DUCK, AND ONE DUCK IN THE MIDDLE. HOW MANY DUCKS WERE THERE IN TOTAL?

TOTALLY gross! ←

"If I ever find out who's writing me these letters then I'm going to fart on their pillow!"

"Will!" Mum scolded. "That's awful!"

"These letters are supposed to help me, so why can't they make it easy?" I whinged.

"Give it here," Zoe said, snatching the letter from my hands.

Captain Luke Solvit and Jamie Solvit peered over Zoe's shoulder, excited to see an Adventurer letter written to someone else.

"Exactly the same handwriting as my letters," said Captain Luke.

"And mine," agreed Jamie.

"Well, isn't that interesting," Grandpa Monty smiled. "The letters are being written by the same person."

"Impossible," I said in a moody voice – I was

Quack! Quack!

still annoyed at my letter. "How can one person drop letters off to people living at different points in time?"

"I've got it!" Zoe shouted. "I know the answer! It's three! Two ducks in front of a duck and two ducks behind a duck and one duck in the middle. How many ducks were there in total? Three – easy."

"She's right you know," said Lord Avalon with a smile.

I ran around the back of Bob the robot and pressed the number three on the keyboard.

"Hello. Master," Bob said in a robotic voice.

I walked around in front of Bob. His eyes blinked and his mouth jerked into a smile. "How. Can. I. Be. Of. Service?"

"Who left the letter in your hands?" I asked quickly.

"I. Did. Not. See," Bob answered. "I. Was. Sleeping."

"Where are we?" Zoe asked.

"Year 9999," Bob said. "Humans. Gone. From. Earth. For. Two. Thousand. Years."

"Where did they all go?" Mum asked Bob.

"Fled. From. Partek. Partek. Control. All. Of. Space."

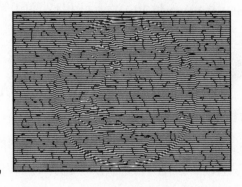

"The Partek control the whole of space!" I shouted in astonishment – how could this have happened?

"I. Wait. Here. For. Master. Of. Time. To. Save. Mankind."

"That's me," I told Bob. "I'm the Master of

Time. But how am I meant to save mankind?"

"Rescue. Henry. From. Partek," Bob said.

"And then what?" I asked.

"Then. Use. Adventurer. Skills. To. Help. Earth."

"Excuse me?" said Captain Drake. "Who has to use their Adventurer skills? Will?"

"Yes," Bob answered.

"Where will we find my dad?" I asked Bob.

"Fly. To. The. End. Of. The. Universe. That. Is. Where. You. Will. Find. Him."

"Are you coming too?" Zoe asked Bob.

"No," Bob replied. "Now. I. Will. Sleep."

The light in Bob's eyes dimmed and his head tilted forwards as he switched himself off.

"Right," I said, trying to process all of the mind-blowing information Bob had just given me. "Captain Drake," I called. Captain Drake stood forward and nodded at me.

"I'm going to turn Morph into a spaceship and you need to fly him to the end of the universe, OK?"

"OK!" he said with a smile. "To the end of the universe we go!"

CHAPTER FIVE
THE TALISMAN'S MAP

It was a super-smart idea to bring Captain Drake on this Adventure. No one could handle a spaceship as well as he could. I knew that as soon as Morph got moving, Captain Drake would take us wherever we needed to go.

"Do you have the coordinates for the end of the universe?" Captain Drake asked me.

"Er...no," I replied. "Can't we just blast off into space and keep moving until we can't go any further?"

"But which direction do we need to move in?" Captain Drake wrinkled his eyebrows.

BRAIN FREEZE! I hadn't thought this out well at all!

"Use the Talisman of Truth," said a voice from behind me.

"Lord Avalon?" I said, turning around and looking at the wizard-looking lord hopefully. "The Talisman can show me which way I need to go?"

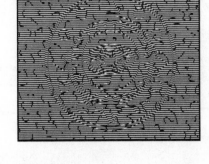

"The Talisman can show you whatever you need to see," replied Lord Avalon. "All you need to do is ask it to show you the way."

Everyone watched nervously as I pulled the Talisman of Truth out from under my T-shirt. I've been wearing the Talisman ever since I became an Adventurer. It works as a key and helps me understand other languages. I had no idea it could work as a map though.

WOO HOO! I LOVE the feeling of travelling through space!

Captain Drake steered Morph through space, weaving between meteors, planets and stars with ease. He was awesome behind the wheel of a spaceship – he made it look so easy.

"Thanks for joining me for this Adventure," I said to Captain Drake. Everyone else was hovering around Grandpa's picnic basket again and I'd taken the opportunity to have a quick few minutes alone with Drake.

"It's my pleasure to help you," Captain Drake smiled. "Henry is my friend. I've known him for many years – it would be wrong of me not to be a part of his rescue mission. Thank you, Will, for giving me the chance to be there. There is one thing we need to do though."

"What's that?" I asked curiously.

"Everyone who hasn't fought the Partek before needs to know what we're up against. You, me and anyone else here who's encountered the Partek before need to warn the others."

"Good point," I agreed. "You get the best results in battle if you know your enemies well." That was something that I'd learnt on many of my Adventures – the more you know about who you're fighting, the easier it is to hit their weak spots and bring them down.

Captain Drake put Morph onto autopilot and we headed towards the others.

"Guys, get comfy," I shouted at everyone. "Captain Drake and I need to have a few words with you all."

"Sounds serious," said Akemi through a mouthful of pickled egg cookie.

"What we have to say is important if we want

to win the battle with the Partek," said Captain Drake.

"No fool goes into battle without wanting to win," said Captain Luke, leaning back against the wall and crossing his arms across his chest.

"Exactly, which is why you guys need to know as much as possible about who...what it is we're fighting," I said.

"These Partek live up here, amongst the stars?" said Lord Avalon.

"That's right," said Jamie, walking up to me and Captain Drake so the three of us were facing the others.

Between us, we told the others everything we knew about the Partek and what they could expect when they met them.

We told them things like this:

The Partek

What they look like:

Can disguise themselves as normal cats. Otherwise, they look like giant cats with sharp claws where their tongues should be.

What motivates them:

Power, universe-domination and wanting to capture me (although who knows why!).

Their weak points:

They hate fish (especially kippers), are not that smart, are very reliant on technology and are easily defeated when in normal pet form.

Their strengths:

Strength, technology, can hypnotize animals, numbers (there are millions of them), disguise.

No wonder... they stink!!

"So how do we find these troublesome creatures?" Mark Antony asked, already ready for battle.

"I don't think we'll have to look hard – they may find us first," I replied.

"From what I've seen of the Partek," Jamie added, "they don't have any mercy, compassion or justice – they fight dirty."

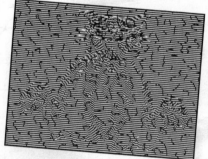

"This is a very dangerous mission," said Akemi seriously.

"I'm sorry that you're all going to have to face what's ahead," I said, feeling guilty that I was taking my friends into such danger. "There's a chance we won't all make it back alive."

Lord Avalon stood up and put his hand to his

heart. "I can't think of anyone I would rather die for, Will Solvit. You are brave and fight for justice and truth – I am willing to lay down my life for those noble causes."

"I shall follow you into death and beyond," said Mark Antony, rising to his feet.

"I trust your leadership, Will Solvit!" said Akemi, standing up.

"We're all right behind you," said Zoe.

"We're gonna show those Partek what a battle is really about," I shouted. "We're going to blow them to dust!"

LET'S DO THIS!!

CHAPTER SIX
A CLOSE ENCOUNTER

Soaring through space is kind of like you'd imagine it would be. All you can see is the pitch-blackness of deep space dotted with stars and colourful nebulas.

"It's totally crank, isn't it?" said Jamie, standing by my side as we both stared out of Morph's windows. Jamie's from the future and uses strange words like 'crank'. "I travel through space all the time," he continued, "but I never get bored of staring out of a spaceship window."

"How's it all going?" I asked Jamie. "Being an Adventurer, I mean." I was lucky enough to be there when Jamie had his first Adventure, and

WILL'S FACT FILE

Dear Adventurer,

I hope you've enjoyed reading about my alien adventures. For thousands of years people have been seeing mysterious objects in the sky, but UFO mania really took off in the middle of the twentieth century. Since then there have been thousands of reports of UFO sightings and alien encounters.

This fact file is packed with cool stuff about aliens and UFOs. Check out the amazing info and then dazzle your friends and family with your knowledge.

Did you know? Most UFOs are symmetrical, smooth and featureless, without rivets or welding seams.

Alien and UFO facts

- Aliens are life forms from another planet.
- The word 'extraterrestrial' comes from the two Latin words meaning 'outside' and 'earthly'.
- Aliens might exist on Mars, Jupiter and Saturn.
- 'Martians' is our word for creatures from Mars.
- UFOs are unidentified flying objects that come from another world.
- Many scientists believe that it is impossible that some form of extraterrestrial life form doesn't exist.
- People who study UFOs are called ufologists.
- There are three categories of close encounters with UFOs.
- Close encounters of the first kind are close sightings of a UFO.
- Close encounters of the second kind are when UFOs affect the environment by flattening trees, burning animals or similar.
- Close encounters of the third kind involve actual contact with aliens.

TIMELINE

Around 12,000 BC
Some cave drawings seem to show a disc-like aircraft.

1482 BC
Egyptian hieroglyphics show a fiery ball seen in the morning sky.

41 BC
A large object, similar to the sun, appears in the night sky over Rome.

15 August 1663
A large flaming globe is seen over a lake in Russia.

23 April 1897
A Kansas farmer reports an airship kidnapping one of his cows.

1933
The ghost planes phenomenon begins.

Autumn 1944
Air crews in Europe and the Pacific report sighting flying balls of light.

24 June 1947
This date is considered the beginning of the flying saucer craze.

July 1947
The Roswell Incident ignites the world's interest in flying saucers and little green men.

1952–1953
A rush of people come forward claiming to have encountered aliens or UFOs.

19 September 1961
Betty and Barney Hill are reportedly 'abducted by aliens'.

1960s–70s
There is a spate of UFO sightings over Warminster in the UK.

1980s
The first crop circles appear in the UK.

2000—Present day
People continue to see and take pictures of UFOs, while others claim to be abducted.

To this day it has not been discovered what the mysterious balls of light were.

Allied airmen spotted glowing balls of light over Europe during World War II.
- They assumed they were enemy aircraft, but they were far too fast and always flew off without a fight.
- They were first seen in 1944 by the US 415th Night Fighter Squadron.
- After the war it was discovered that the Germans had also seen them.
- American band the Foo Fighters is named after the sightings.

In the 1930s mysterious 'ghost flyers' were spotted over Scandinavia.
- Sometimes they shone dazzling searchlights on the ground.
- They were normally alone but sometimes came in pairs or groups.
- They performed amazing aerial acrobatics and flew far faster than any other known aircraft.
- They were impossible to shoot down.
- Ghost rockets were spotted in 1946.

Ghost flyers were huge, grey aircraft, bigger than anything flying at the time.

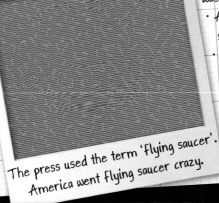

The press used the term 'flying saucer'. America went flying saucer crazy.

The term 'flying saucers' was first used in 1947.
- An American pilot, Kenneth Arnold, spotted mysterious objects in the sky.
- Arnold assumed it was some sort of super-duper top-secret aircraft.
- The technology of the aircraft clearly wasn't of this world.
- In Arnold's words, 'They flew like a saucer would if you skipped it across the water'.

The now-famous Roswell Incident put UFOs on the world stage.
- On 4 July 1947 radar staff at Roswell Air Force Base in New Mexico spotted an unknown aircraft.
- The incident was forgotten until 1978 when a retired major said that the military had covered up what really happened.
It was claimed that UFO debris was collected and alien bodies found.

UFO fanatics still claim that the military covered up a UFO crash.

In the 1960s and 70s a quiet rural town in Wiltshire became the site of some sort of mysterious phenomena.
- Strange sounds made one witness feel weak and unable to move.
- A photo of a UFO hovering over the town was published in the Daily Mirror.
- Warminster became a UFO hotspot.
- Some people believe the sightings were of experimental aircraft from a nearby military training centre.

A cigar-shaped ship, covered in lights, was seen on different occasions.

In November 1952 George Adamski was the first person to report coming face to face with an alien.
- He said a humanoid with long blond hair emerged from a spaceship.
- The alien communicated through telepathy and hand signals.
- Adamski even maintained that he was taken on a trip in their spacecraft.
- He became an international celebrity.

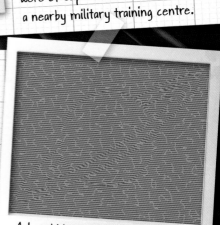

Adamski later claimed to have met other aliens from Saturn and Mars.

The Suttons from Kentucky reported aliens attacking their farm in 1955.
- They said that a naked glowing figure about 1 metre tall approached them.
- It waved claws over its head.
- It was blasted down with a shotgun, but walked away unharmed.
- More intruders appeared.
- The encounter was taken seriously enough to be investigated by the United States Air Force.

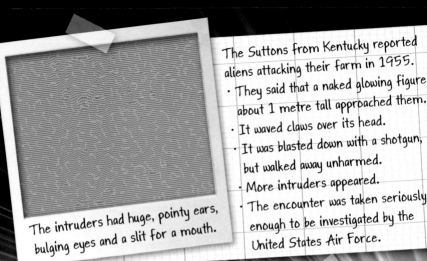

The intruders had huge, pointy ears, bulging eyes and a slit for a mouth.

In 1961 Betty and Barney Hill spotted a pancake-shaped UFO in the sky.
- Later they realized they had lost two hours of time.
- After suffering from disturbing dreams, Betty and Barney underwent hypnosis.
- The hypnosis showed that they had been abducted by little grey aliens who had subjected them to medical experiments in their spaceship.

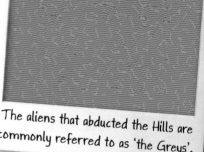

The aliens that abducted the Hills are commonly referred to as 'the Greys'.

When news of the Hills' abduction got out, other people came forward.
- Abductees are often said to be taken from a car or bed.
- People are returned to the exact sam spot they were taken from.
- Victims say they are poked and prodded with various instruments.
- Some describe having implants surgically implanted into their bod

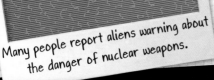

Many people report aliens warning about the danger of nuclear weapons.

Since the Roswell Incident, governments and scientists have investigated UFOs.
· Many US investigations found no evidence of extraterrestrial visitors.
· The 1969 Condon Report concluded that aliens didn't exist.
· This ended the US government's official investigations into UFOs.
· The UK's UFO investigation unit was closed in 2009 after 50 years.
· Secret investigations still go on.

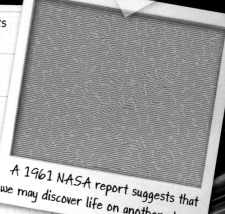

A 1961 NASA report suggests that we may discover life on another planet.

By gathering information from abductees, ufologists have been able to build up a picture of your average alien.
· They may vary from little grey men to human-like reptiles.
· They likely have extensive and advanced knowledge of psychology.
· They seem to be telepathic.
· They seem to have strong mind-control powers.
· They are secretive about their plans.

Some experts believe that aliens would look more like a bug than a human.

Alien technology is believed to be far more advanced than anything on Earth.
· Aliens seem to control gravity and make people levitate (float).
· UFOs and aliens may be able to pass through solid objects such as walls.
· Aliens seem to disable guns and make machines, including cars, malfunction.
· They may have a shield that can make themselves and their ships invisible.

Their airships seem to be capable of flying at ridiculously high speeds.

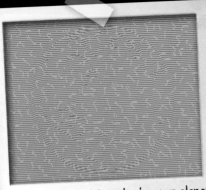

If aliens are so great, what do they want from Earth? Here are just a few theories.
· They want to breed hybrid babies that combine the very best alien and human qualities.
· They want to obtain some of our valuable minerals.
· They just want to study us out of inter[...]
· They want to feed off our emotions.
· They want to improve and develop us.

They might want to colonize our planet because they are running out of space.

UFOs and aliens are held responsible for all sorts of unsolved mysteries.
· Many people think that crop circles are messages from extraterrestrial beings.
· Mysterious mutilation of cattle and horses has been blamed on aliens.
· Disappearances of ships and aircraft around the Bermuda Triangle could actually be alien abductions.
· Some legends say aliens helped to create Stonehenge!

The Nazca Lines in Peru may have been for gods visiting Earth by flying saucers.

E.T. (1982) is the story of a little boy who befriends a cute alien.

There are plenty of films for UFO fans to enjoy.
· Close Encounters of the Third Kind (1977) is about a man whose life changes after an encounter with a UFO
· Independence Day (1996) is a sci-fi movie about a hostile alien invasion of Earth.
· The Star Wars movies are full of aliens.

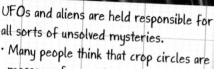

I was eager to learn how he was taking to the Adventurer lifestyle.

"Being an Adventurer is beyond crank," he smiled at me. "I can't imagine doing anything else."

"I know what you mean," I agreed. It was good to have another Adventurer there to talk to, especially one my age – even if Jamie was my great-great-great-grandson! "I can't imagine ever giving up Adventuring," I told Jamie. "I never want to retire like my grandpa Monty's done."

"What makes you think Monty's retired?" Jamie asked with a confused expression on his face.

"Of course Grandpa's retired," I said, looking over at Grandpa trying to feed Plato a yogurt-coloured crab stick. "There's no way he can still be a spy."

"I wouldn't be so sure," Jamie whispered.

Really? Could Grandpa Monty be going out spying when I was at school each day?

"Will!" I heard Zoe shout from the other end of Morph. "Will, come and look at this."

I left Jamie by the window and headed over to Zoe. She was standing by what looked like a cupboard door.

"It's locked," Zoe said, pointing at the door. "And I don't remember this being here when I got into the spaceship earlier."

"Maybe it appeared as Morph expanded," I suggested. It sounded crazy, but trust me – when it comes to Morph and dark energy, anything's possible.

"Do you think your amulet would fit the lock?" Zoe asked with a twinkle in her eye. She knew that it would – it was exactly the right shape and size.

She is annoyingly smart!! ☺

I pulled the Talisman of Truth out from beneath my T-shirt and held it over the lock of the cupboard door.

Sure enough, the lock clicked and the door sprung open.

The cupboard was empty except for one white envelope sitting on a shelf.

I picked up the envelope and quickly read the letter inside.

WHAT'S AN ASTRONAUT'S FAVOURITE DRINK?
GRAVI-TEA!

THERE IS MORE THAN ONE PARTEK SPACE STATION AT THE END OF THE UNIVERSE. DON'T WASTE TIME BY LOOKING FOR HENRY IN ALL OF THEM – GO STRAIGHT TO THE SPACE STATION HE'S BEING HELD IN.

THE STATION HAS THE NAME OF A ROMAN GOD.

THE GOD HAS THE NAME OF A PLANET.
HIS WEAPON WAS A SCYTHE.

"Mark Antony!" I yelled loudly, without even thinking about it.

"Yes, Will?" the Roman army general called, making his way towards me. "How can I be of assistance?"

"How's your knowledge of Roman gods?" I asked him, passing him the letter.

"I don't read your language," he said, looking down at the letter. "Only Latin I'm afraid."

"Of course," I said. "Sorry." I quickly translated the clues in my letter to Mark Antony. I'm so used to the Talisman of Truth around my neck translating foreign languages for me that I always forget which language I'm speaking! "From what

I know about planet names, Mars, Venus, Saturn, Jupiter and Neptune were all named after Roman gods."

"Saturn carries a scythe," Mark Antony replied confidently. "He's the god of time."

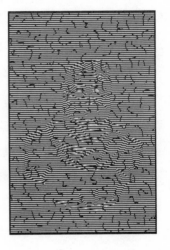

"Thanks," I smiled.

Before I could say anything else, something crashed into Morph and I found myself knocked on to the spaceship floor.

"What's going on?" Mum cried in panic.

"We're under attack!" Captain Drake called back from the control decks.

"Battle stations, everyone!" Jamie called.

Mum, Grandpa, Lord Avalon and Zoe all rushed

to man Morph's laser guns, ready to fire at our enemy.

Jamie and Captain Drake stayed at the front of the ship, managing the control decks and keeping the spaceship on course.

Akemi, Mark Antony, Captain Luke and I all waited by Morph's spaceship door – poised with weapons and ready to fight if we needed to.

Another laser blasted us from the right and Morph shook from side to side.

"It's the Partek!" Captain Drake cried.

"How many of them are there?" I yelled.

"There's only one ship," Jamie called back. "And they're...they're...they're retreating."

"**WHAT?**" Zoe screamed, taking her hands from the laser gun trigger and throwing them into the air in shock.

I knew how she felt. Something was up. There

was no way the Partek would run away from us unless something was up. They loved to fight.

"Maybe they've run out of fuel?" Jamie suggested.

"Or they're just scaredy cats!" Zoe giggled.

"I say we chase after them and see what's up?" Jamie suggested.

"We don't want to veer off course," Mum chipped in.

I thought about it for a moment. "I think Jamie's right. There's some reason that the Partek on that ship don't want to fight us, and I want to know what it is."

"As you say," said Captain Drake, hitting the accelerator and blasting after the Partek spaceship.

We chased the ship through deep space. It didn't take long for us to catch up with it. As we were closing in, the alien spacecraft plummeted downwards, leaving a trail of smoke behind it.

"It's going to crash-land!" Jamie shouted in horror.

Sure enough, the Partek ship smashed into a meteor below.

Captain Drake lowered Morph down through the sky and prepared to land on the meteor.

"I'm going to park Morph as near to the Partek ship as I can manage," Captain Drake said, bringing Morph in to land. "Then it's up to you to go out and see what's going on," he said to me, Mark Antony, Luke and Akemi – the warriors of the army.

"OK, let's get suited up." The four of us quickly put on our spacesuits (I put my Aztec mask on underneath mine, just in case). By the time we were all ready, Morph had landed.

"Be careful, Will." Mum kissed the top of my spacesuit as I headed into the decompression chamber.

The door to the outside world slid open and we stepped out onto the rocky surface of the meteor.

The Partek ship had crash-landed just in front of us.

We nervously walked up to it, expecting it to fire lasers at us, but it didn't.

Something was definitely up.

The door to the spaceship had smashed open on impact. With the other three behind me, I led the way into the alien spacecraft.

I couldn't see anything at first because there was smoke from the crash everywhere.

As soon as the smoke cleared, I could see that the inside of the ship was tiny – there was only

the one small room we were standing in. There
was only one Partek in there. And he was staring
straight at me.

NOT
a pretty
kitty!

CHAPTER SEVEN
BRAVERY AND MERCY

"What is that beast?!" screamed Akemi.

"Partek!" the injured Partek spat back. I'm no doctor, but I could tell that the Partek in front of me was badly hurt. It was lying on the ground and had shrunk down to normal cat size.

The Partek let out an angry hiss. It sounded like a cross between a snake and a screaming tiger. There's something about the sound of Partek voices that sends shivers up my spine.

"Will Solvit!" the Partek spat at me.

"How does he know who you are?" Captain Luke asked in astonishment. "We've travelled far into the future and are at the outer limits of the universe. How on earth can he recognize you, Will?"

"Every Partek knows Will Solvit!" the Partek hissed at me with evil in its eyes.

"Why? How?" I asked angrily, determined to find out once and for all why the Partek seemed so obsessed with me.

"I won't tell you our secrets," the Partek cried, wincing in pain.

"He's injured," Mark Antony said, edging closer to the Partek to get a better look.

"I'd say his legs are broken," confirmed Captain Luke, bending down and squatting at the Partek's level.

"Arghhhhh!" the Partek screamed at us, partly in pain and partly because he hated us being near him.

"If you could get back to your city then the rest of your stupid kitten race could help you," I said, cooking up a plan in my head.

"He's not going anywhere," Luke said. "His legs are broken and his spaceship is beyond repair."

"We could take him to the Partek city ourselves," I said calmly.

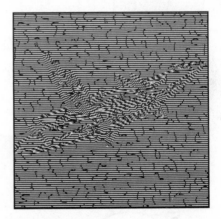

"WHAT?" Luke, Akemi and Mark Antony screamed at the same time, in their different languages.

I bent down and looked into the Partek's cat-like eyes. It hissed at me and let out a pathetic meow in pain.

He was right. For the first time since I'd embarked on this Adventure I realized that I was heading straight into a death trap – and I was taking my friends with me.

"Why me?" the words caught in my throat. I coughed to clear my throat and then spoke louder. "Why are the Partek going to so much trouble to capture me?"

"You are important, Will Solvit," the Partek said in a muffled voice, before howling in pain. "But that's all I know," it pleaded. "I promise, I don't know any more than that."

"I think he's telling the truth," Luke said quietly to me.

I stared at the Partek at my feet, who was whimpering in pain. It was a symbol of pure evil – it was part of a race that had captured my dad, imprisoned my mum and were trying to kill me –

not to mention all the planets they'd destroyed.

But I was true to my word. The Partek may be lying, cheating villains, but I'm not – and I wanted to show them that.

"OK," I said to Luke, Mark and Akemi. "Carry him out of here and into Morph."

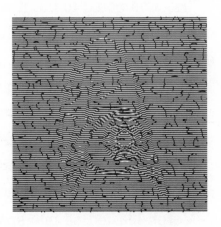

They didn't argue and did as I said.

"What are you doing!" shrieked Zoe in disbelief as we walked into Morph with an injured Partek.

"Put it down there," I said, pointing to a bit of floor that the Partek could lie on. "Grandpa, got any more food we could feed this little kitten?"

Grandpa Monty nodded and started to rummage through his picnic basket.

"Did you have your mind sucked out in space?" Zoe asked through gritted teeth, storming towards me.

"He was going to die if we left him there," I explained to Zoe. "I'm not like them – I'm not evil."

"If you think that helping this...thing...means the Partek are going to show you mercy, then you're wrong," Zoe shouted at me.

"Ready for take-off," Jamie shouted from the front of the ship.

Morph blasted off into space and away from the meteor that we'd landed on.

"If the coordinates are correct," Captain Drake called back to me, "we'll arrive at our destination in just under an hour."

I was NOT going to be like them!!

My stomach tightened into a painful knot. There was only an hour left before I had to face the whole Partek race, and only an hour before I arrived at where Dad was being kept prisoner.

Captain Luke, Akemi, Mark Antony and I all started to take off our spacesuits.

"Well done, Will," Akemi said, reaching out and putting a hand on my shoulder. "You did the right thing. It is braver to show mercy to your enemies than to leave them to die."

"Thanks, Akemi," I said, peeling the Aztec mask from my face.

Akemi and Mark Antony headed off to speak to Zoe and calm her down.

Grandpa Monty and Jamie headed over to me. We gathered in a circle with Captain Luke.

"Look at this," Grandpa said with a broad smile. "Four Adventurers in one spaceship!"

AWESOME!

☹ Nightmare!

"I wish I knew what I was meant to do," I said glumly. "It seems that whatever decision I make, someone's not happy."

"That's the burden you must bear when you make difficult decisions," Captain Luke said gently. "Commanding an army has never been an easy thing to do."

"You can say that again!" I joked.

"At least we have our letters to help us in our Adventures," Jamie said cheerfully.

I pulled my latest letter out of my pocket and looked at it. "I wish the letters were more helpful," I complained. "Sometimes they can be a total pain to work out."

"Can I look at that?" Captain Luke said, taking my letter from my hands. "It's all just so odd," he frowned. "I'm convinced that the handwriting in this letter is exactly the same as in my letters."

Mmm? Something REALLY weird is going on! 84

"It's definitely the same as mine, too," Jamie added, leaning in to get a closer look.

"Well, it's been a while since I've had an Adventurer letter, so I couldn't possibly say," Grandpa said, shifting his weight from one foot to another. I looked at him with narrowed eyes, remembering what Jamie had said to me about not believing that Grandpa was retired.

"Maybe the letters are all written by the same person?" Jamie suggested.

"That's impossible," Captain Luke snorted. "How can one person leave letters for people who all live in different centuries?"

"They'd have to have a time machine," Jamie replied.

"Well as far as I know," I said, taking my letter back from Luke and folding it up again. "Only my dad can build time machines and he can hardly be the one sending letters when he's held up in a cat prison, can he?"

'That's not your father's handwriting," Grandpa said confidently.

"Well, whoever is writing the letters," I said, "is going to have a lot to answer for when I finally get hold of them, that's for sure!"

I left the small group of Solvit Adventurers and headed over to Zoe. Whatever Mark Antony had said to her had obviously worked because she seemed to have calmed down.

"I'm sorry I didn't trust you, Will," she said.

"That's OK," I said, looking down at the injured Partek who had fallen asleep on the spaceship floor.

"I think he fainted," Lord Avalon said. "He was in a lot of pain."

"Destination is on the radar!" Captain Drake

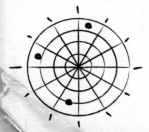

shouted from the command desk. "Everybody prepare to land. We're heading towards the Partek city!"

CHAPTER EIGHT
THE CITY AT THE END OF THE UNIVERSE

Everyone stood side by side at the front of the spaceship. At first, the Partek city in the distance just looked like a white blob in the middle of space, but as we got closer, it became clearer.

The city was a collection of dark, black space stations that stood near each other. There were various bridges connecting the different stations together – it reminded me a bit of a fancy cage that you'd keep a hamster in.

"Home," growled the injured Partek behind us.

"What are we going to do with him?" Zoe asked me with worry.

"We'll just drop him off," I answered. "Hope that one of the other Partek can help him."

We were really near to the city. I could make out small Partek spacecraft flying between the different stations.

"This is madness," Jamie said with panic. "We're literally strolling into a city of Partek!"

"Like lambs into a lion's den," said Lord Avalon gravely.

"I've activated Morph's invisibility shields," Captain Drake informed everyone calmly.

"We need to find the Saturn space station," I reminded Captain Drake, who was steering Morph in between two large Partek spacecraft.

"Will," Jamie said to me. "Can we ask our Partek companion where the Saturn station is? I don't fancy our chances of flying about for hours trying to find it."

"You hear that?" I shouted back to the injured Partek, waking him. "Where can we find the Saturn station?"

"It's next to the Felix station," it replied in a tiny whimper, too tired to argue back. "Felix is the gold station in the centre of our city."

"Thank you," I said. "We'll drop you off there for you to get help."

Captain Luke steered towards the large gold space station floating in the middle of the city.

I could hear everyone take a sharp intake of breath as we began to weave our way through Partek spaceships and space stations.

"They're not attacking us," Mum said with worry in her voice. "Why aren't they attacking us?"

"We want you to come to Saturn," said the injured Partek. "You're falling right into our trap."

"And they can't see us, remember," I reminded Mum. "Morph's invisible."

Mum let out a nervous giggle. You could tell she wasn't used to Adventuring.

Morph soared along the side of the magnificent Felix station. It was shaped like a diamond and had hundreds of docking ports in its side that alien spaceships were flying in and out of.

"That must be Saturn there," pointed Captain Luke.

There ahead of us was a small black space station shaped like the face of a cat.

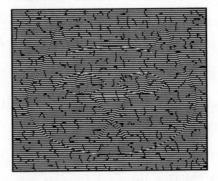

"What do you want me to do, Will?" Captain Drake said gently, looking at me for an answer.

"Pull in to the docking bay at the space station," I replied. "If it's me they want, then it's me they'll get. I've figured out what I'm going to do. I'm just going to put my invincibility mask on and walk straight in there. I want to avoid a battle. There's no way we'd win. We're surrounded by Partek – they'd blast us to dust."

Captain Drake steered Morph into a docking bay in the side of the Saturn space station.

"This is it, guys," I said bravely. "This is why we came here – to face the Partek."

Suddenly the darkness in the tunnel was flooded by a piercing white light.

Morph came to a standstill and Captain Drake turned the engine off.

"Mark Antony, Captain Luke, can you help me carry the injured Partek out with me?" I said, bending down to pick up my bag of Adventure tools. I took out the pot of invisibility paint and threw it over to Luke. "Cover yourselves with this," I said. "I don't want the Partek to know you're there with me. Everyone else stay here – I've got to do this alone."

"Be careful, Will," cried Mum, rushing over to me and giving me a suffocating hug.

"Good luck, old boy," said Grandpa, shaking my hand.

Everyone else wished me luck and I headed towards the spaceship door.

I opened the door and stepped out onto a white platform. Mark Antony and Luke followed me.

There were three Partek standing on the platform, all waiting for me.

"What are you?" the Partek hissed at me.

"I am Will Solvit," I said in my bravest voice. "I've come here to find my father."

BIG mistake!

"You don't look human," the Partek in the middle snarled.

"I'm wearing my warrior mask," I said proudly. "Do anything you want to me – it won't hurt."

I probably shouldn't have said that.

The Partek let out a thrilled hiss of delight. "We shall certainly try..." one of them said.

"Is this your prisoner?" another one hissed.

"No," I said, as Luke and Antony lowered the injured Partek to the ground. "I brought him here because he was hurt, so you could help him."

"Will Solvit is telling the truth," the injured Partek said. "He rescued me and brought me here."

"Very well," the Partek in front of me huffed. "Take him off to the healing station," he instructed the two Partek by his side.

"I'll take it from here," I said quietly to Antony

94

and Luke, so the Partek couldn't hear.

"Good luck, Will," they whispered back.

They both headed back to our invisible spaceship, leaving me alone with the Partek.

"You will come with me, Will Solvit," the Partek growled at me. "I will take you to our leader."

Was I doing the right thing? Was I on my way to rescue Dad, or was I walking to certain death?

There was only one way to find out.

"Lead the way," I said to the Partek. "I'll follow you."

CHAPTER NINE
HENRY SOLVIT

So there I was. Alone in the Partek city, at the end of the universe in the distant future. I'd left my friends and family behind in an invisible spaceship and was walking along with my greatest enemy – the Partek.

And the reason for this brain-numbing craziness = rescuing my dad.

"How do I know that you'll let my dad go free?" I asked my Partek guide as he led me through the corridors of the Saturn space station. The Saturn space station was nothing like the DARE Satellite, which is run by humans. The place was filthy, as if it had never been cleaned.

Total stink-fest!!

It smelt of rotting meat and cat litter.

"Your father will go free," the Partek growled at me. "It is you we want, Will Solvit. And now we have you."

"Fine," I said bluntly, trying to stay calm.

I was playing along with the Partek, making them think that I'd surrendered to them, so that I could rescue Dad. Of course I intended to escape once Dad was free. I just hadn't worked out how I was going to do that yet...

I was led to a large door at the end of the corridor. The door seemed to be made out of wood, which was odd as everything else looked so new and futuristic.

The Partek raised one of its front paws and pushed the wooden doors open.

The doors parted to reveal a dimly lit hall with wooden floorboards and wooden walls – it looked more like a garden shed than somewhere a leader of a powerful alien race would be.

I looked around the hall desperately, trying to see my dad.

Then I heard his voice. "Will, you shouldn't have come here," said the voice.

"Dad?" I stepped into the room and something fell on me from above.

A net!

I tried to wriggle free but the more I struggled the more tangled I became.

"ARGH!" I cried in frustration.

"Your father is right, Will Solvit," growled a deep voice from the shadows. "You should have never come here. In fact..." a shape moved in the darkness, and I could see it walking towards me, "...you should never have become an Adventurer in the first place."

The biggest Partek I'd ever seen slunk out of the shadows and padded towards me. It was huge – about twice the size of a lion, I'd say. Its eyes glowed like burning coals and its sharp tongue hung from its mouth, ready to attack at any moment. On its furry head sat a crown made of jagged space rock. I knew that the Partek before me was the leader of their race.

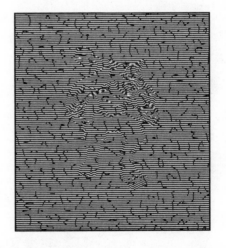

"I want you to release my dad!" I demanded, too angry to care how important the Partek in front of me was.

"Bring Henry forward," the Partek instructed.

"I am brave, Dad!" I argued. "I've been on loads of Adventures and every one of them has been a success."

I was panicking now. I had no idea what Dad or the Partek was talking about. What kind of responsibility was too much to handle? Why did other Adventurers depend on me? I was only a kid!

"I don't understand," I uttered quietly.

"It's you, Will," Dad said simply. He was inches away from me on the other side of the net, and I could see his face trembling as he told me the truth. "You're the one that writes the letters."

WHAT!!! WHAT!!! WHAT!!! WHAT!!!

"What?" I managed, not sure I'd heard right.

"It's you, Will," he repeated. "When you're older, you use your time machine to travel through time and leave clues for every Adventurer to

This was making my head hurt!!!

find. Without the help of your clues, no Solvit Adventurer could ever have solved mysteries and saved the world from evil."

"That can't be true," I argued, feeling my face turn red and air tightening in my chest. My dad was talking rubbish. He had to be. How could one person leave hundreds of letters throughout time? "Impossible."

"Yes," the Partek said with a laugh. "It will be impossible for you to travel through time and help other Adventurers once you're dead. And no Adventurers means no protection for Earth. The history books for your world will tell a very different story as soon as you're dead."

I stared into the face of my enemy as its clawed tongue flicked around its mouth with excitement. Suddenly everything seemed to make sense, and I understood why the Partek wanted me dead so badly.

Thoughts of Jamie, Captain Luke and Grandpa crossed my mind. I thought of all the other Solvit Adventurers who had ever lived – the people whose statues and portraits decorated Solvit Hall. I was the one who wrote their Adventure letters. I was the one who led them into battles and helped them fight evil. Without me and my letters, the world was doomed.

A feeling of bravery rose within me, a feeling stronger than anything I'd ever felt before. I knew how important it was for me to survive – the history of mankind depended on it.

Taking a deep breath, I stood up tall.

The Partek was walking towards me, a wicked grin spreading across its furry face. "Will Solvit," it hissed, its scaly tongue reaching towards me, poised to strike. Out of nowhere I felt its tongue swipe at my face and knock my mask off.

How was I going to escape from this one?

The Partek leader held its tongue up, ready to strike again. "Prepare to die."

This was bad...
REALLY BAD!!!

CHAPTER TEN
ESCAPE

The clawed tongue swiped towards my throat like the crack of a whip. It was a hair's width from my skin when suddenly it froze in mid-air.

There was a loud crash as the Partek leader fell stiffly to the floor.

"Stun gun," said a voice that sounded a lot like Zoe's. "I found one in Morph's secret cupboard."

"Zoe?" I gasped, looking around for my best friend who had just shot the leader of the Partek with a stun gun. She was nowhere to be seen.

"I'm invisible," she said. "I thought I'd come and see how you were doing – and it looks as if you could do with a bit of help. Hurry up." I heard her move towards me and felt her fingers begin untangling the net. "Luke, Akemi and Mark Antony are holding off the guards at the door but they won't be able to for long."

"They're invisible too?" I asked.

"Of course," she replied.

Dad rushed towards me and pulled what looked like a pencil from his pocket. "Stand back," he ordered Zoe. The pencil in Dad's hand began to turn a bluish colour before flashing like a lightbulb. Dad held the pencil up to the net, and the net suddenly fell to pieces. "It's my new atomizer," he said proudly. "It breaks anything down into atoms in under a second!"

I'd missed Dad and his crazy inventions.

I lunged towards Dad and threw my arms around him. "You're safe," I muttered.

"Will, we don't have time." Zoe tugged at my

arm. "We need to get out of here – fast!"

"Well said," agreed Dad.

We headed towards the wooden doors.

As we walked out into the corridor, I could hear Mark Antony shouting loudly. "Get back, beasts!"

"Hi...ya!" shouted Akemi, as I saw his samurai sword fly through the air and take down the Partek. Akemi had obviously forgotten to cover his sword in invisibility paint.

"Truly amazing," Dad smiled at me. "You brought these people here, Will?"

I nodded. "They're part of my army."

"The others are waiting in Morph," Zoe told us. "Take this." She threw a stun gun at me and a supersonic screecher at Dad. "You left your Adventure bag back on Morph. I had enough paint to cover the bag up but not everything inside it," she explained.

Dad stared at Morph with wide-eyed wonder. "Oh, Will," he said. "You've done me proud."

"There really isn't time for this, Mr Solvit," Zoe said in her politest voice. I could tell she was panicking though.

We piled into the spaceship.

"Henry!" Mum shrieked, tears streaming down her face. She ran towards Dad and threw her arms around him tightly. Then she grabbed me and pulled me in to the hug.

At last – I had my family back!

I felt a tug at my ankles and looked down to see Plato biting at my trouser leg.

"Hello, boy," Dad said, bending down to ruffle Plato's fur. "Dad!" he shouted over at Grandpa Monty. "What are you doing out here in deep space?"

"I brought the sandwiches," Grandpa Monty

smiled, giving Dad a hug. "It's good to have you back, son."

"Everyone prepare for take-off!" Jamie called. "Everyone who's invisible, do me a favour and quickly wipe yourselves visible again. We all need to see each other if we're going to work together to survive. We've got a rough ride ahead."

Jamie wasn't wrong.

Getting out of the Partek city was about as easy as trying to stuff a watermelon up your nose.

Morph was shot at from every angle. Our spaceship may have been invisible, but the Partek knew we were there, and they didn't want us to leave!

"Put the kipper defence shield up!" Dad advised Captain Drake.

"Morph has a kipper defence shield?" Drake

I need this for Grandpa's cooking!!!

asked.

"The only thing that will keep the Partek away," Dad said. He reached down and knelt below Morph's control deck, pushing a button that I'd never even seen before.

Zoe, Lord Avalon, Mark Antony and Akemi all manned Morph's laser guns, and between them they shot down any alien spaceships we passed.

"They're following us!" Captain Drake shouted desperately, as we zoomed into deep space with the Partek city far behind us. "We're not going to lose them. They're too fast."

"We'll lose them if we travel back through time!" Dad suggested.

"How can we do that?" I said with worry. "We're using Morph as a spaceship. We can't use it as a time machine at the same time!"

"Of course you can," Dad said simply, as if I

was just asking how to stand on one leg. "Morph can do whatever you want it to!"

Dad strolled over to the control deck without a worry in the world. "Allow me," he said to Captain Drake.

Captain Drake stood back, eager to see what Dad had planned.

Dad tapped something into Morph's control deck and then turned around to look at me. "Hold on to your stomach!"

I felt Morph lurch forwards and groan like a whale. Suddenly the skin on my face began to ripple and my stomach knotted itself. It was a feeling I was more than familiar with – time travel!

By the time Morph had stopped time travelling I was sitting on the ground.

"You OK?" Zoe said weakly. Her face looked

seriously green.

"Yeah, you?" I replied.

"I think I might be sick," she answered.

"Where are we?" Captain Drake asked Dad.

"Don't you recognize where we are?" Dad smiled at his old friend.

I looked out of the window and immediately saw the DARE Satellite.

"DARE!" Captain Drake cried in disbelief. "If

we're back at the DARE Satellite then we must have..."

"Travelled through time and space to drop you off on your doorstep," Dad finished. "Thank you for your help, Drake."

"Not at all," Captain Drake replied. "It was my pleasure."

We dropped Captain Drake off in the docking bay of the DARE Satellite.

"Thanks again," I smiled at him. "See you soon!"

"We did it!" Zoe smiled as Jamie flew Morph back into space. "Your parents are finally home and we escaped from the Partek."

"Yeah," I agreed.

I suddenly remembered everything Dad had told me back in the Partek city. About how it had been me all along who had written the letters.

I looked around at the other Adventurers in the room – at Luke and Jamie and Grandpa and wondered if they knew. Should I tell them it was me? Was I meant to keep it a secret?

The thoughts whirling around inside my head were almost too much to bear. I felt as if my head was going to explode all over the spaceship floor.

Grandpa Monty shuffled towards me on his walking stick. "You OK there, David?"

"I'm Will, Grandpa," I replied. "I'm OK. I've just had a bit of a mad day, that's all."

"How about we drop your friends off and then go home to Solvit Hall for a cup of cocoa and a good old chat?"

"That sounds great, Grandpa," I said.

One by one I dropped my friends off and thanked them for their help.

Morph travelled back to ancient Rome and I

116

said goodbye to Mark Antony. The next stop was ancient Japan where I waved goodbye to Akemi. Then we travelled to medieval Avalon Castle where I thanked Lord Avalon for showing me how to use the Talisman as a map. Next we dropped off Captain Luke.

Zoe was the last person we said goodbye to.

"You must come over soon for dinner," Mum smiled at Zoe.

"I'd love to, Mrs Solvit," Zoe replied as she headed into her house.

"Such a pretty, pretty girl," Mum said to me.

MUM!

CHAPTER ELEVEN
THE ADVENTURE IS ABOUT TO BEGIN

I went straight to bed as soon as I got back to Solvit Hall. I was exhausted. "We can talk about things in the morning, darling," said Mum as she kissed me goodnight.

"No more secrets," I yawned as my eyelids fluttered closed.

I was woken up the next morning by the smell of pancakes tickling my nose.

I went downstairs, and Grandpa Monty, Mum and Dad were sitting round the breakfast table. I paused for a moment in the kitchen doorway, rubbing my eyes to check I wasn't dreaming.

What I was seeing was real. Mum and Dad were home – we were a family once again.

"Good morning, son," Dad smiled, pushing a plate stacked high with pancakes towards the empty seat at the kitchen table. "Hungry?"

"Starving!" I replied, sitting down next to the steaming plate.

"We have maple syrup, bacon and eggs, jam, sugar and chocolate sauce for the pancakes," Mum grinned.

"Or I've made a fresh eel and apricot glaze if you fancy it," Grandpa added.

"Um, I'll have eggs please," I replied. I couldn't stop smiling.

"I can't believe we're all together again," I said through a mouthful of pancakes.

"Listen, Will," Dad said seriously. "I have some, er, rather bad news."

"What?" I asked suddenly, my mind racing with possibilities: aliens, zombies, curses...

"I'm afraid we can't go home just yet," Dad said. "I drove back to our old house after you'd gone to bed last night to pick up a few of my things. Only our house wasn't there any more – it's been brought to the ground."

"What do you mean?" I asked, confused.

"According to the neighbours," Dad continued, "there was a gas leak in the house – a super-strength fart gas leak – that ignited and blew the house up!"

I nearly spat my pancakes over the table in disbelief. Only in my family would a leak of super-strength fart gas bring down a house.

"So you'll be staying here with me!" Grandpa Monty smiled.

"Cool," I added. "I mean, it's cool that I can

live near Zoe, and I kinda like living here with you, Grandpa."

"I like you being here too, Will," Grandpa said, remembering my real name.

"I'm going to convert the West Wing of Solvit Hall into a laboratory," Dad said, sipping a cup of coffee. "I'm keen to get back to my research and experiments!"

"And I'll be here to help Stanley around the house while you're at school during the day," Mum smiled.

"Whoa!" I said loudly. "School? I can't go to school. I have to fulfil my destiny and travel through time to lead Adventures."

"You can do that in the evenings and on weekends," Mum said sternly, "so long as you do your homework first."

Not fair! Not only did I have the responsibility

of hundreds of Adventures on my shoulders, but I had to go to school as well!

"After you're back from school today," Grandpa smiled, "I'll show you an old spy trick of mine that will help you disguise your handwriting."

"Why do I need to disguise my handwriting?" I asked.

"You can't let people know it's you writing the letters," Dad replied. "Especially the letters you'll send to your old self. Imagine your confusion if you received a letter in your own handwriting before you knew what was going on!"

Dad did have a point.

"Finish your pancakes and then get dressed for school," Mum said.

I quickly gobbled up my last pancake and rushed upstairs to get washed and dressed.

Thoughts of all the letters I'd received rushed

122

through my head like a speeding train. I thought about the very first letter I'd ever received. I was in detention at my old school and I found a letter between the pages of a book about dinosaurs.

I remembered how excited I'd been, how all I wanted to know was who had sent me the letter and what it meant.

As I was packing up my school bag, a thought struck me. That evening, as soon as Grandpa Monty had shown me his old spy trick to disguise handwriting, I was going to go back in time and leave that letter for myself. I planned it out as I walked down the stairs of Solvit Hall, passing the portraits of my ancestors with my school bag slung over my shoulder. I'd go back to the classroom half an hour before I started detention, and I'd sneak in and leave the letter between the pages of the book.

"Have a good day," Dad said, smiling at me as I walked towards the front door.

Mum pushed a brown paper bag into my hands. "Some sandwiches for lunch."

Mum kissed me goodbye as I climbed into Stanley's car. The car rolled away from Solvit Hall, and I turned around and watched Grandpa, Mum and Dad wave me off.

We drove down the mile-long driveway of Solvit Hall and I stared at the statues of all the Adventurers who had lived before me. George the Egyptologist, Caroline the deep sea diver, Clifford the explorer, Sebastian the astronomer and Edward the mountaineer. I was going to travel to some amazing places, and probably meet some incredible people as I travelled through time to lead the Solvits on their Adventures.

For some reason I always thought that as soon

as I found Mum and Dad my Adventures would be over, but now I realized that they were only just getting started.

My mouth opened into a wide smile and I let out a small chuckle as I thought about the first letter I'd be sending to myself that evening...

WHAT WAS THE SMELLIEST DINOSAUR?
THE STINKOSAURUS!

The adventure is about to begin...

Check out
www.will-solvit.com
for more about my mega-cool
time travelling Adventures!

OTHER BOOKS IN THE SERIES